T0147818

DIAMOND

DIAMOND

A WOMAN OF THE GREAT MIGRATION

JANICE STARGHILL KEEL

DIAMOND
A WOMAN OF THE GREAT MIGRATION

iUniverse books may be ordered through booksellers or by contacting:

iUniverse
1663 Liberty Drive
Bloomington, IN 47403
www.iuniverse.com
1-800-Authors (1-800-288-4677)

ISBN: 978-1-5320-4994-1 (sc)
ISBN: 978-1-5320-4995-8 (e)

Library of Congress Control Number: 2018905891

Print information available on the last page.

iUniverse rev. date: 07/03/2018

RUTH 1:16

And Ruth said, intreat me not to leave thee or to return from following after thee; for whither thou goest, I will go; and where thou lodgest, I will lodge: thou people shall be my people, and thy God my God.

The Holy Bible – King James Version, Thomas Nelson Publishers

Acknowledgments

Photograph – A Shipbuilding Tradition –
Kaiser Shipyard Memorial,
Vancouver, Washington pp. 63,64

Photograph – A Shipbuilding Tradition –
Kaiser Shipyard Memorial,
Vancouver, Washington, pp. 65,66

With great thanks to the real women of the Great Migration who shared their stories with me.

Dedicated to: Carter, Smith and Starghill families.

CHAPTER

1

I represent my generation and feel great humility that I lived through World War II, and helped to build an aircraft carrier that was launched from the shipyards of Vancouver, Washington in the 1940's. I survived the great depression, segregation, and Jim Crow. The first man who walked on the moon was during my lifetime. I have had the pleasure to witness our people finally obtaining civil and voting rights. I have seen the Model T and horse drawn wagons on the street and now the computerized cars and vehicles to explore space. Through all phases of my life, I can say "God is good". I am a 96-year-old woman who was born in the United States of America and have always lived here and always supported this country for better or worse. Looking back at my life to share my thoughts and experiences with my family, so they can be recorded and shared as a part of our history. I will share with you the stories my Mother, Marie Carson Hilton and others told me of my birth and early years, and then I will share my memories of my life. A good life!

Marie was the middle daughter of Alice Carson. She had an elder sister, Cynthia who was kind, compassionate, and gentle and a younger sister, Jean who was fiery, fractious and difficult. Marie, hard worker, loving and kind was often mediator. Cynthia married Robert Johnson and moved away to start her family. Marie, Jean and three brothers, Harrison, Wesley and Luke lived with their Mother, Alice in Meadow View, Virginia.

Marie Carson and Alonzo Bryson were teenagers who fell madly in love. When they found out that Marie was expecting, Alonzo wanted to marry Marie. However, that was not to be because Alonzo's parents had other plans for his future and would not allow the marriage to take place. They sent him away and broke-up the romance. Marie was left pregnant and broken-hearted. The only man she would truly love left her feeling not good enough for his family or him. It was considered disgraceful to become an unwed mother in Marie's community. It was a different time from our total acceptance of single mothers today.

Cynthia heard of her condition and invited Marie to come and live with her and Robert, during Marie's pregnancy. Marie was delighted to go and live with Cynthia. She loved and respected Cynthia and knew she was kind, loving, and would welcome her and her unborn-child into her home. Marie was much happier away from the scornful, accusing eyes of the neighborhood people in Meadow View, Virginia. Cynthia and Robert had been married for many years at that time and they had a young daughter, Mae Hester. They moved to Algoma, West Virginia from Meadow View, Virginia around 1917, so they had not lived there very long before Marie came to live with them in the middle of her pregnancy. On December 14, 1918, I was born in Algoma, West Virginia at Aunt Cynthia and Uncle Robert's home. Mama said I was her jewel and named me Diamond.

Harrison Carson, Marie's oldest brother migrated from Meadow View, Virginia to Rolfe, West Virginia soon after Cynthia and Robert moved to Algoma. Rolfe was not very far from Algoma. Harrison invited Grandmother, Alice Carson and his younger siblings to live with him. Alice (I called her Mama Carson) invited Mama and me to come and live with her and Uncle Harrison shortly after my birth. When we moved to Rolfe I was a new born baby girl and my mother, Marie who was born in 1900 would have been around 18 years old.

It was a good move for Mama because Rolfe is where Mama met her future husband, John Hilton. Mama was twenty years old, John was twenty-five and I was two years old when they met. There were many young women chasing John who was a very eligible bachelor. One woman in particular was so very much in love with John and pursued him very aggressively. She hounded his door until John made it abundantly clear that he loved Marie and only Marie, and he proposed to Mama and they were married. John gave me and Mama his name. He was a wonderful stepfather and made me feel like I was his own.

I was told that Mama stood a stately 5'5", beautiful figure, dark chestnut brown soft, smooth skin. She was known to everyone because of her beautiful legs. She was articulate, worked hard and always well dressed. She loved keeping up with fashions of the day through magazines and worked hard so she and I could live well. Because she was well read and very adept socially many of my teachers believed she was college educated.

John was tall, handsome, neat, trim and highly favored. He was a self-taught engineer, and clothing salesman. He sold suits and shoes to the local men. He measured and ordered custom clothing for them and for himself. He supplied tailor made suits for his customers, and he was a barber and cut their hair. I guess he was a full-service entrepreneur. The men did not enjoy going to town to shop because of segregation in the stores that did not allow black people to try on the clothes. Consequently, John had plenty of orders for their clothing needs. John was bi-racial and looked so European that he could not be identified as a black person without his birth certificate. If the situation required him to pass for white to help his family acquire food when they travelled, he would do so. He could go in the front door of a white only restaurant and order food that he would take out and share with Mama and me. He received freshly cooked food, instead of going to the back door where they may or not sell to colored people, and if they did sale to colored people it would be stale. He worked hard to provide for Mama and me and did all he could to make us happy.

My first memory of my childhood was in 1925 when I was seven and living in Rolfe, West Virginia with my Grandmother, Alice Carson and my Mother, (Marie Carson Hilton). Mother came to Rolfe to visit Mama Carson and to enroll me in school. Before 1925, I had been living in Tralee, West Virginian with my Mom and Dad. Tralee was an isolated rural area and did not have a good school for so called "colored" children that was in walking distance. Mother was afraid to allow me to go to the colored school because it was seven miles away. It would have been necessary for me to walk seven miles to school at the age of five. I did not go to school at all until after she took me to live with my Grandmother and I started school at Rolfe.

Mama was happy for me to start school there. She taught me at home to read and to do arithmetic before I moved to Rolfe, so when I started school I was very advanced for Kindergarten. I could read everything in the primer, *Baby Ray* and answered all the questions related to the book and could do the math. I was immediately promoted to first grade. Mama loved to read, so she spent hours reading stories to me and taught me to love to go to school and love learning. When I passed to second grade the following year, the second-grade teacher decided to promote me to the third grade immediately. After I had adjusted to my new school, Mama went back home and I stayed on with my grandmother and continued my education.

When I moved to live with Grandmother, Uncle Wesley, lived there with his younger sister, Jean who was 19 and 14-year-old brother, Luke. Although, Luke was my uncle we were more like brother and sister. We went to the movies together every Saturday. Rolfe had an all-black movie theater and an all-white movie theater in our neighborhood. We went to the neighborhood theater most of the time and occasionally we went downtown to a building that was divided in half to accommodate segregation in the theatre. No one liked going Downtown to the theater because of the invisible line separating the races. White people on one side and black people on the other side. Segregation was legal in West Virginia, so the races were required to be separated in every way possible. There were two entrances to the movie theater. Blacks entered on the left and whites entered on the right. We could see the other side that was all white but could not sit on that side of the aisle. The refreshment stand was in the center and was segregated. There was a window on the left to service colored people and a window on the right to service white people. There was a black ticket taker on our side. I do not know what was on the other side because we were not allowed to go there.

The Rolfe neighborhood was divided with black coal miners on a portion of the main street and many of the white coal miners on the hill. Some of the white coal miners preferred the hill because they were accustomed to living in the mountains. Middle class whites lived further down the main street from the coloreds. The white elementary school was a beautiful two-story building and the black school was one story and very ordinary. There was always a difference in size and convenience. The black school was primary thru 6th grade. I do not know anything about the white school since we were not allowed to go there. There was a corner restaurant, (company owned) managed by Mr. Rade, a very stingy black man. He sold ice cream, candy and gum to the kids. Ice cream was five cents a cone, but he would try to give us the smallest dip of ice cream possible. I remember how angry we were because we felt we were cheated by our own. He was a great company man with little regard for his own people.

There was a playground with swings, a merry-go-round and seesaw across the street. Nanny and Grady Prince would take over the playground and not let anyone they did not like on the playground. They would kick, and curse and make kids leave. Even back then there were bullies who would make the lives of others miserable. They would let me stay because they enjoyed visiting my house to play with my toys and eat candy, and they always protected me at school. Nanny and Grady had chores to do before they could come out to play, but as soon as they finished with their chores they would come to the playground and make most of the other kids leave. There were six swings. They would not let anyone else swing. I did not like them but had to get along with them to survive. They used very foul language against other children, which made us cringe.

My grandmother, Alice Carson ran a boarding house for single coal miners who came to work in our town. She had accommodations for three boarders. There were three beds in a large room that was shared by the boarders. She provided food and housekeeping. Aunt Jean was the cook and Mama was dish washer and housekeeper whenever she was there. Boarders paid $7.00 a month so they did not add a lot of money to the household budget. Although bread was five cents a loaf, eggs ten cent a dozen, most of the money was spent on food for the boarders. She managed her tight budget. The boarders supplied her main source of income.

Uncle Harrison, moved to West Virginia in 1918, after he was hired to work in the coal mines. Over time he was promoted to brakeman in the coal mines. Digging and loading coal was a common job that was done by "colored" men in those days. (We were called "colored".) In the past, the motorman and brakeman were skilled trade jobs and usually "whites" were hired for those positions. Somehow Uncle Harrison gained the respect of the owners and was trusted to have the very prominent position of brakeman. He was killed in the mine shortly after he was promoted to brakeman. Many people believed that the motorman had caused his death. The motorman complained about working with a colored man, and it was rumored that the motorman was a member of the "KKK". Consequently, when Uncle Harrison was killed there was some whispering about who may have caused his death, but nothing came of it.

After Uncle Harrison's death Mama Carson kept the house and stayed there with her younger children. Wesley Carson (Big Wesley), the second born son was a teenager when Harrison died but later when he came of age he went into the coal mines to work. He became a brakeman and later he was promoted to motorman for the mine. During Uncle Wesley's employment as a motorman, a white guy named Mike was his brakeman. Mike was killed and Uncle Wesley brought his cold, dead body out of the mine on the coal car. There was such an uproar because the whites believed that Wesley had something to do with Mike's death. Rumors spread that "Wesley killed Mike in the mine".

Soon after Mike died, the colored coal miners heard rumors that the KKK was coming to their neighborhood that night to kill Wesley. They quietly spread the word for all the men to stay up all night with their guns and put the women and children to sleep on the floor. Our neighbors armed themselves quietly. They were very "hush, hush," about what they were doing and quietly waited for the KKK to come. I was a little girl staying with my grandmother, but I can remember it was a scary night for all the little kids. I slept on the floor snuggled as close to Mama Carson as possible and cried silently throughout that night. No one slept. The next morning it was clear that the KKK did not show up. The men put on their work clothes and went to work.

We found out that the Company put out a warning to the white miners that anyone participating in any trouble would be fired and driven from their homes. Wesley was not prosecuted. The Company said officially that Mike's death was an accident.

CHAPTER

2

Mama worked as a domestic to help supplement our family income. She had to leave our family to stay at the home of her employer and take care of their family. One of Mama's employers asked her to bring me to work with her. She wanted me to play with her daughter who was near my age. These were white professional people who did not allow their daughter to play with the nearby white children of the coal miners. This was so ironic that after I became an adult I asked Mama about this and she surmised that her employer thought it was better for her daughter to play with me because I would never be considered her social equal. Mama believed her employer felt the white coal miner's children weren't good enough. She did not want any association that might lead to true friendship. Classism existed along with the racism in our community. I went with Mama to work only once because she could not watch me while she worked, and she did not want me to be used.

When Mama came home on the weekends John would cook breakfast, pick her up and carry her into the kitchen and prepare her plate. He treated her like a queen. He knew what a big sacrifice she made to leave her child and husband to care for another family. When I became older I realized that Mama was not as in love with John, as he was with her, or as I thought she should have been. John wanted to have babies, but she had a tumor and was afraid to go to the hospital. When she finally went to the doctor it was too late and she needed a hysterectomy. Although I was his step-daughter, John treated me like his blood. Mama appeared jealous of my affection and did not want to share me with John. Sometimes, John would take me to the movies, so we did have some father/daughter time together, but Mama wanted all my affection. She felt left out of our daily lives and cheated out of her motherhood.

Mama had the surgery in 1927 and afterwards she and I moved to Bluefield, West Virginia so she could work. In 1929 we moved back to live with John when I was 11 years old. He drove to Bluefield to pick us up. We thought he was "sharp" with a green suit, shirt and tie to match. Apparently, my parents had been communicating without my knowledge. He told Mama about the house he had waiting for us and took us home. He had a job in Amanita, Virginia. It was a nice coal mining village. New houses on both sides of the street because this was a new coal mine. John was a coal miner now to support us, but he continued his other enterprises. The town had paved roads and cement sidewalks. It was a nice place and Mama liked living there. John rented a house, with two bedrooms, living room, dining room, kitchen and pantry. Everything was on one floor. When we got there, John had furnished the house with a plush couch, two chairs, and a floor model radio in the living room. The bedrooms were furnished with comfortable furniture as well.

Mike Jones was the owner of the coal mine and the fuel company. In those days before a coal mine opened, housing was built for the workers near the mine. Consequently, the company owned everything and provided everything depriving the workers of the opportunity for entrepreneurship.

I had a bedroom all my own and was afraid to sleep in the room alone. So, I slept on the living room couch, outside my parent's bedroom door. I was a nervous wreck. I would get in the bed with them anytime I felt afraid. I would scream "I am scared" and one of them would come and get me. I became a brat who did not sleep in her own bed. If someone died I would be scared for weeks. I slept with them until I was 13. At thirteen I decided I wanted to sleep in my room, hopped out of their bed and never returned. Now that I think back on my behavior I know that they should have sent me back to my bed, but my parents allowed me to control their bedroom. I feel as though my immature behavior may have ruined their marriage. When I married and had babies, my husband told me "no babies in the bed at night". I could play with the babies in our bed, but the babies had to sleep in their own beds.

When we stayed in Amanita, West Virginia, I attended public schools 6th – 8th grade. While there I was active in the drama department. I played many lead parts in school plays. I attended AME Methodist Episcopal Church and sang in the Youth Choir and attended service every Sunday. My parents were very loving and kind and provided me a nice home, clothes and spending money. My parents worked hard together to insure we always had financial security.

My two best friends were Edna Hairston, my pastor's step daughter, and Annie Preston. We would go to school socials and house parties where they would play big band music on the radio. My friends called me "Chick" because I was short and light on my feet. We listened to Cab Calloway, Earl Hines and others and we would dance to their music. Two of the big bands, Duke Ellington and Cab Calloway came to our school. The boys wanted to watch the musicians use their musical instruments and the girls wanted to dance. We went to basketball games and had lots of fun being young. Maxwell Benson was my boyfriend at that time. He was tall, handsome, with a medium brown complexion. I thought he was so good looking. We went to movies and dances and I thought he would be my future husband. We decided to wait to come of age before getting serious.

Again, in ninth grade I went to stay with my grandmother at Rolfe and started school there that winter. Grandmother had been very ill and needed someone to stay with her. She was arthritic and her youngest daughter, Jean married Melvin (Buddy) Brown and moved to Glen Alum, West Va. Before I agreed to go to live with her I made her promise me that she would not die while I lived with her. I had a great phobia of the dead. I loved Mama Carson, but she had to promise me that she would not die while I lived with her. She promised that she would live a very long time, I felt relieved about living with her and agreed to live with her as long as she needed me.

In my mind, I can see Mama Carson as I remember her, tall, slender, medium brown skin, middle aged woman with long dark hair pulled back into a tight bun. She walked unsteadily and wasn't able to work due to arthritis in her joints. Her hands were stiff and twisted, which prevented her picking-up anything. Her knees were stiff, causing much difficulty when she attempted to walk. Over the years Mama Carson had given birth to six children: Harrison, Cynthia, Marie (My Mother), Wesley, Jean and Luke. Her health had deteriorated over the years. When I arrived to live with Mama Carson and my uncles, Wesley and Luke, she was totally disabled.

Wesley was a fun uncle who taught me how to dance. He was really a great dancer and loved to dance as much as I did. He would put my feet on top of his and whirl me around the room. He was so much fun and very patient with me. I loved music so much that I would jump up from the dinner table and start dancing when one of my favorite songs played on the radio. I confess I was pretty much allowed to do whatever I wanted to do while growing up. Ironically, I became a strong disciplinarian with my children.

While living in Rolfe my friends and I rode the train to Norfolk High School because that was the only means of transportation to the high school. There were two high schools in Norfolk, one for whites and one for coloreds. We all rode the train because there were no high schools at Rolfe. The whites rode in the "white only" cars and the coloreds rode in the car set aside for us. McDowell County sent checks for all the kids (white and colored) to take the train to Norfolk High Schools. All the families worked in the mines and rode the trains owned by the mines. People were transported on the same tracks that transported the coal out of the mines. The train was the main public transportation. Only a few people had motor cars. The only other public transportation was a bus owned by Mr. Jeter a white man who allowed colored and whites to ride together. There was no discrimination on that bus. If you paid your fare, you could sit in any seat available on the bus. It was limited to mostly inside the coal mining neighborhood.

Our school transportation checks arrived the first of the month to cover the train rides to school for the month. One month we decided to walk to school and keep the train fare to buy new clothes. There was no place for young people of color to work and money was scarce. We arrived on time to school every day, but somehow the County caught on to us, and the next semester the County sent us train tickets instead of checks.

As I grew older I had a serious boyfriend, Leonard Smith at Rolfe. He was older and a chauffeur and handyman. We had fun times together. He worked for an African-American Doctor who let him use the car. On Sundays, we would go for long drives or a movie. He planned to be my future husband. I loved guys with ambition and I liked to go places, so I thought Leonard was perfect for me. I had some great girlfriends which included my best girlfriends, Pauline Griffin, Dorothy Gamble and Frieda Satterfield. When I was not with Leonard I was with these friends. We went to school together and had so much fun attending parties.

CHAPTER

3

Mama Carson allowed me to go home in 1935 to live with my family when I was in tenth grade. The next year after I started the 11th grade I endured one of the greatest shocks of my life. This particular morning, I awoke with a "Happy-go-lucky" feeling, without a care in the world and then I was told that Mom and Dad were separating. It was a bomb shell exploding in my mostly happy, carefree life. I tearfully asked Mama, "What are we going to do? Where are we going to live?" I was heartbroken and devastated.

My parents separated in July 1936. They sold the furniture and all the things they owned and divided the money. Mama and I moved to Bluefield, West Virginia. Mama had worked in Bluefield before and thought her experience would help her find a job there. She got us a studio apartment which we rented from Mrs. Hancock a widow who owned a nice brick house on the main street in the city. The apartment house was in the rear of her home.

Mom and Mrs. Hancock wanted me to continue my education. I had been out of school because of the move and did not want to go back. I would have been completing 11th grade. I felt like my Mom could not support me alone by doing domestic work. I didn't have time to think about what I really wanted to do with my life.

Unknown to me, Nathaniel Stuart saw my picture on the mantel over the fireplace at Aunt Jean & Uncle Buddy's home in Glen Alum, West Virginia. He became very attracted to me through that picture and wanted to meet me. He was acquainted with my Aunt and Uncle at the church in Glen Alum, and volunteered to drive them to Amanita, VA. Mama Carson shared time living with my family and their family. Jean and Buddy wanted to take Mama Carson back to their home to live with them for a while. Mama Carson had been staying with us for several months. I had gone to a school social and wasn't at home when they arrived, so Nathaniel's plan to meet me fell through. Sadly, we did not meet.

When I arrived home later that night Mama asked me to guess who was here?" She told me that Jean and Buddy came to pick up Mama Carson, and the young man who drove the car wanted to meet me. She said, "I'm so happy you weren't home because I do not like the idea of him intruding". I was excited and wanted to know more about the young man who drove over 100 miles to see me. She tried to play it down but did tell me that he was handsome and tall. Soon after his visit my parents separated.

After my parents separated and my Mom and I were on our way to Bluefield, West Virginia to live, I asked Mom if we could stop by Glen Alum to see Mama Carson before we moved to Bluefield. I had an urge to see my grandmother because I feared that It could have been a long time before I would have an opportunity to see her again. Mama agreed, and we went to Aunt Jean and Uncle Buddy's house where Mama Carson was staying.

When we arrived in Glen Alum Nathaniel came over to my aunt's house to meet me. I will never forget when he drove up in a 1935 beige Chevy. He was a coal miner, young, tall, handsome with a beautiful tan complexion that turned bronze during the summer sun and I was very impressed with him. I was totally captivated by him. He took me out to the local restaurant and bought ice cream. The girl he was dating happened to be out of town on vacation, so he was free of her, but her mother made herself known. He ignored her. He told me he lived with his parents to help his Dad care for the family. He was the 12th child of 15 children. His parents were old and still had children and grandchildren to raise. They lived in a large 8 room house on a hill. His two brothers, three sisters including an older sister and her two children lived there.

Before Mom and I left for Bluefield, West Virginia, Nathaniel asked me to write to him soon and let him know when he could visit me. We did not own private telephones, so we corresponded by mail. He came to visit me the next weekend and proposed to me during that visit. He told me about his religious convictions, and that he had prayed for God to help him find a wife. He was to become an ordained deacon at the Baptist church and felt that it was time for him to marry, if he was to remain true to his religious commitment. He hadn't found anyone that made him happy. Then he told me about seeing my picture on the mantle at my Aunt's house and a voice telling him "That is your wife".

We liked each other immediately, so when he asked if we could go on a date; I said yes. I wanted to see him again. I felt that God had sent him to me at a time when I did not know which way to turn. On our first date, he said "Diamond, you are my wife". I was shocked. I said, "I have to think about this". He said, "I am serious! I want to marry you; I know you have boyfriends, but I am serious, and I am not taking any chance that you may marry someone else".

After he left I told Mama that he asked me to marry, and she did not like it. She did not want me to leave her. He came to visit the next weekend and asked Mama if he could marry me and she was furious and said a loud resounding, "NO". I talked to her and asked her to think about it. I told her that this man wants to marry me and take care of me. I told her that "I don't know how to work", and I reminded her that she could not take care of me working as a part-time domestic. Nathaniel and I made plans for our wedding during each visit. Nathaniel came several weekends and each time I talked to Mama and wore her down. She finally consented, but we had plan "B". If she had not consented, we would elope.

He had similar problems on his end. His family was against the marriage as well. They told him that "you don't know that girl". They did not want to insult the Campbell family whose daughter he was dating. The Campbell girl and her parents were very close to Nathaniel's parents. She called his parents, "Mom" and "Dad". Although, they were not formally engaged, the families felt they would eventually marry.

It is possible my life may have been different, if my parents had not separated. I had planned to marry a local young man, Leonard at Rolfe. He was waiting for me to come of age. He just happened to be out-of-town driving his employer when all this occurred. There was no way to communicate since we did not have telephone service. When Leonard came home it was the eve of my marriage and he heard the news that I was engaged to Nathaniel. He came directly to my house and while I tried to explain to Leonard why I was marrying someone else, Nathaniel drove up. My young cousin, Charles Johnson ran into the kitchen shouting your boyfriend is here. Charles was a little boy then, but he would tease me about saving me from getting caught with Leonard in the kitchen. He thought it was hilarious that Leonard had to leave out the back door. I never saw Leonard again. However, Leonard's cousin came to the wedding and cried throughout the ceremony and asked me afterward, "How could you do this to Leonard?"

CHAPTER

4

athaniel and I planned a small wedding ceremony for November 24, 1936 at my grandmother's house in Rolfe. We met in August and were married in November. Nathaniel asked if I wanted a big wedding, but I said no. I remembered a neighbor, Lucille who was jilted by a man from Mingo County. She had planned a huge wedding and the groom did not show up. Ironically, Nathaniel was from Mingo County and he knew the absent groom, so he understood why I wanted to keep the wedding a secret. No one was invited until the wedding day when Uncle Wesley went out into the neighborhood inviting people to come. I invited only family.

Nathaniel came up the day before the wedding and spent the night at our house. He slept in the bedroom with Luke, who was one year older than Nathaniel. They remained good friends after the wedding. I remember Uncle Wesley, Ollis and Pauline Gamble (our witnesses), family and a few friends being there. We had a very small wedding. Aunt Jean and Uncle Buddy were not there even though they were responsible for our meeting. I wore a blue dress trimmed with grey and Otis wore a blue suit. There were no photographs because Mama and I were in such disarray after moving from Amanita to Bluefield that we could not find the camera. When I married Nathaniel, I had known him for only three months. We met in August and married in November. I liked him a lot, but I cannot say I was in love so quickly. I hoped love would grow with time.

After the wedding ceremony, I stayed at home with my grandmother and Nathaniel went home that night. He had to work the next day. He had planned for me to go back with him, but allowed me to stay because grandmother asked if I could stay with her until my birthday. I would turn 18 years old on my birthday in December. She talked him into letting me stay. My grandmother, Alice Carson ran my life all of her days. She had a little story ready for Nathaniel. She told him that the marriage was so quick that she needed time to get use to the idea. He relented and said I could stay, but he would pick me up on the day after my birthday and that I better be packed and ready to leave. Nathaniel was swamped by my family throughout our marriage. They always tried to tell me what to do. We had a little private time together and then he left. My grandmother sent my husband away without me. I felt disappointed but knew he would come back for me.

Before Nathaniel left home to come to our wedding, he told his family "I'm getting married". They did not believe him. His Mother, Cathy said jokingly, "Who would marry you? No one wants to marry you." And laughed at him. He drove away that morning and planned to bring back his wife. When he drove home after the wedding, his younger sister, Lilian looked out the window to see if he truly had married and was bringing home a bride. When he came in alone, they asked him, "Where is your wife?" He replied, "I have one, although she is not with me". His mother told him to show her a marriage license, and he did. They were astonished and speechless.

December 15, 1936, the day after my birthday Nathaniel came for me and I was ready to leave with him. Everybody in town was waiting for him to come for me. Uncle Wesley was so proud that I was married to a fine young man. He told everyone in town that Nathaniel was coming to take Diamond to his home. Everyone watched out their windows as we left on our journey from Rolfe to Glen Alum, West Virginia which was to be my new home.

Glen Alum hollow was a small coal mining village that was in the hills of Mingo County. The actual town was Williamson. Houses were along the road side leading to the coal mines. There was a large company store, post office, restaurant, and there was one small theater.

When we arrived in Glen Alum I was so nervous that I was almost shaking. Everyone waited to see me. I could see people peeking out their windows. Mama Cathy, Kitty, her two girls, Matthew, Thomas, Lillian (baby girl) and Papa Stuart were all standing near the door when we walked in. They welcomed me into the family, but they were a little suspicious of me because I was the big city girl who had stolen their son's heart.

The Stuart family had a large two-story, eight-room house. The back was level to the ground, but the front of the house was on stilts. The house was painted a white that looked dirty from the road. There were five bedrooms all on the second floor. They had a guest room that was always ready for visiting ministers who came to preach at their church. This guest room became ours. The room was very nice. Kitty, the eldest sister kept the house spotless. We stayed with Nathaniel's family for three weeks and then moved into our home. Nathaniel rented a three-room house close by. He told me he paid for furniture for our house and all I needed to do was go to the store and pick out what I wanted. I was so blessed to move into our newly decorated home to start our life together.

Upon my arrival at Glen Alum I was overwhelmed with the height of the women in my new family. I felt I had moved to the land of the beautiful Amazons. Almost all the women and men (except one) were at or near 6 ft. tall. My father-in-law and I were the only short people in the family. Although Papa Stuart was short he was so regale that he walked tall. It was over powering for me. I was in awe when I walked into my husband's family home and saw my new family.

At eighteen-years-old I was 4'11" and weighed under 100 lbs. I have a dark brown complexion and long thick black hair that I wore wavy and brushed to one side. I was considered very pretty and had no lack of confidence. I was outspoken and had a very strong will to do what I thought was important. I had to learn to live with my husband's family. One thing my new husband and I had in common that helped to create a strong bond between us was the desire to improve our lives and not to get stuck living in a coal mining town forever. We both had the same dream of one day living in Detroit, Michigan and making good wages, and living in a nice house where we could raise our children. I read in the newspapers about the jobs in Detroit, and ironically, we both wanted to live there some day.

There was Mama Cathy, Nathaniel's mother who was 6 feet tall and raw boned, mulatto with silky brown hair which hung to the middle of her back. She had grey eyes, and always wore a scarf on her head. She was very pretty but looked older than her years because she wore long dresses that reached her ankles. She was a wonderful seamstress who made her own clothes both dresses and suits out of cotton prints, but she was, also, a timid, bashful woman, who talked very little. She was sickly and weak after bearing 15 children of which two had passed away and one her first born son, Mark, whom she had before her marriage to Wilbert Stuart, ran away to pass for white and was never seen or heard from again. She had a hole in her heart since he left that was never filled. My husband never forgave his half-brother for hurting his mother and denying his family. His dislike was cemented when Mark did not come back for Mama Cathy's funeral.

Papa Stuart (Wilbert I) was a warm, friendly and studious man. He was short, medium built, with dark, almost black skin, and straight black hair which was cut close to his head. He was a minister for the Mt Zion Baptist Church in Glen Alum. He was very well-dressed and a man with great presence. He had farmed in Georgia before moving to West Virginia.

In the late 1920's Papa Stuart had a cotton farm in Covington, Georgia where they lived in a stately house with a bunk house behind it that housed 30 farm hands and he had stables and a corral for 40 mules to help harvest his crop. He was able to provide a good life for his wife and children.

He taught his boys the business of farming and sent his girls to school, so they could have a good education. He did not believe in educating boys for anything other than farming, so he prepared his boys to farm the land and expected a bright future. Around 1932 the boll weevil infestation ruined his cotton crop and his stubborn refusal to change his crop after three years of infestation caused him to lose his money and his farm. He was forced to leave his family and go work in Oklahoma as a ranch hand to support them. He sent money back to Cathy and the children. He hated being separated from his family. When the opportunity came many years later, for him to work in the coal mines and provide a home to bring his family together again, he jumped at it. He worked as a coal miner and trained his sons to work in the mines. He knew he was responsible for their safety, so he trained them well. Coal mining was the only work available to them at that time, so they followed him into the mines.

Coal was called black diamonds because of it's color. It sparkled like a diamond and was just as valuable. There were million-dollar mines. Factories in the Northern Big Cities were fueled by coal energy. When Papa learned that he could make a living working in the coal mines and that housing would be provided for workers' families he found work and moved his family from Covington, Georgia to Kentucky where the coal mines were located. When the work slowed down in Kentucky he moved to Glen Alum and sent for his family to join him there. His married adult daughter, Georgia and her husband, Bob Munson moved to Glen Alum earlier and informed Papa about the new tunnel mine and that there was housing and opportunity to work.

He preferred to work in tunnel mines. Papa felt that the shaft mines were too dangerous, so he was delighted to find work that was fairly safe to support his family.

When Papa arrived in Glen Alum he rented a large house on a hill. His son's houses surrounded his home. Henry, the eldest brother and his wife, Maggie lived in a house on the left side of Papa, and my husband and I lived on the right side. Bob and Georgia lived below us. The rest of the family lived in the big house with Papa and Mama Cathy. The pay was fair, and the company treated the miners fairly well, so they settled in as a coal mining family.

CHAPTER

5

There was a young woman, Jane Underwood who had a two-year-old baby boy, Paul and was not sure who had fathered the child. Unfortunately, she had been used by most of the young men in Glen Alum so there was great speculation as to the father. People began to suspect that one of the Stuart boys was the father of her child. There were three Stuart brothers of age at that time and they were Henry, Nathaniel, and Matthew. Unfortunately, when I arrived in Glen Alum after such a short courtship and quick marriage to Nathaniel, many people thought I was pregnant. They did not know how wrong they were. Our marriage was quick, but I was not pregnant.

Little did they know that we did not consummate our marriage until after I arrived in Glen Alum. The Amazons (sisters-in-law) immediately began to ask me when I planned to have a baby. I remember one instance when all the family was together; Maggie, Henry's wife asked me "when are you having a baby" and I asked her "when are you having one, since you have been married two years". My other sisters-in-law fell out laughing at her. Maggie never asked me again and she never gave birth to a child.

Jane Underwood left her baby with her step-mother and moved to Charleston, West Virginia to work but never brought anything for her baby when she came to visit. She appeared to enjoy her freedom and lifestyle in Charleston, so she gave care of the child to her step-mother.

Her actions made her seem uninterested in her son. Uncle Buddy and Aunt Jean offered to adopt the boy, but the sisters-in-law insisted that no one could adopt their blood. Mama Cathy and my sisters-in-law did not want the baby neglected because there was a possibility he was a Stuart, so they tried to convince me to raise the child. When I refused they hatched a plan to share raising the child among the three sisters. He would stay a few months with each of them. They wanted to shame me into raising the child. Lillian the younger sister was the "ring leader" and wanted to keep the baby in the family, but she soon tired of the baby. She came by to see me and told me, "Diamond, I understand why you did not keep this baby. This is a lot of work. I am planning to get married and I want to have my own babies." This arrangement did not last long. Shortly after our conversation, Lillian married Albert Butler and started her own family. Her first born was a fine baby boy, Albert, Jr. My old, sickly mother-in-law, Cathy was left to raise the boy.

On December 23, 1937 my first baby, Wilbert II, was born. He was conceived in March and was born in December. Mama came to stay with me and help me while I was pregnant. I had babies at home in those day. I woke up with pain in my back and my mother told me that was a sign that labor had begun. She sent for the Doctor to come for the delivery. I was in labor most of the day. The Amazons wanted to see the baby as soon as it was born, so they came to my home while I was in labor and camped in my kitchen. I could hear them laughing, talking and drinking coffee while I was suffering labor pains. Mama and Nathaniel's Mama were there to help me and that was enough people to be in our home. I often wondered why Mama, or Mama Cathy did not ask them to leave. It was impossible for me to give birth while they were there. My labor began on Sunday morning and I did not have the baby until Monday morning when the women had to go home to get their husbands off to work. During that time, the house was quiet, and the baby came. The doctor stayed with me the whole time. I was so glad they left and were not the first to see my baby.

I believed they wanted to compare my baby with the boy, Paul. They thought my baby would look just like Jane's baby. To my surprise my baby boy, Wilbert II had a fair complexion and auburn hair. They were total opposites. Mama Cathy said my baby was identical to Nathaniel when he was born. They thought I would "mark" my baby by the other boy and that I hated the other child. I could not hate a child, but It was not my responsibility to take care of another woman's child. This woman was healthy and quite capable of taking care of her child. Nathaniel discussed this child with me before he proposed marriage, so I was aware of the child. I told Nathaniel that I would never take care of another woman's child. He never asked me to buy anything for that child when I bought clothes for our baby, Wilbert. I told Nathaniel he could marry the other woman and raise her baby or leave them out of our life. He agreed that he would not mention them again. I know in my heart that I would have taken my baby and gone home to my family.

I was not jealous of this other child that was rumored to be fathered by one of the Stuart young men. The mother had no idea who fathered the child. We learned she named some other man, not a Stuart, on the birth certificate. I may not have been as compassionate as I could have been because I was young, but I wasn't allowing anyone to force me to accept responsibility for a baby that was not mine. My interest was to have my babies and to raise them with my husband.

My husband saw the boy's step-grand-mother struggling to carry him down the street. The Grandmother asked him to buy a baby stroller to transport the boy. Nate agreed, and did not tell me about the purchase. When the bill came in I complained to the store regarding the purchase. When I asked Nathaniel about the stroller he admitted he bought the stroller for the baby. I told him to never make another purchase for that child and to my knowledge he did not. I think about it now and feel I could have shared with this baby who was not at fault.

CHAPTER

6

I felt at home in Glen Alum after living there for more than a year and delivering my first child. Life in Glen Alum became beautiful because I loved my husband and our baby; although there was nothing to do or anyplace to go other than church on Sundays. However, I had reconciled myself to the fact that I loved my husband, and this was the home he provided for me and our children. I still hated that there wasn't much social activity and I was accustomed to parties and school socials. I hated that we were so far into the mountains that I could not pick up any of the radio stations I listened to at home. The only stations we could pick up played blue grass music and I wanted to hear jazz. Mama Marie was a fan of the Grand Ole Opry radio show that was popular those days, but I always preferred jazz. I told Nathaniel that I did not like this part of the world, but I loved him. My love had grown and now I could not imagine life without him.

On a typical day, I took care of my baby, cooked dinner and waited for my husband to come home. When he came home from the mines he would go straight to the shed in back where he kept a huge tin tub used for bathing. He would fill the tub with water every night, so it would be ready when he came home. He would bath and put on clean clothes before he entered the house. His work clothes never came into the house. I was lucky to have this man who was so thoughtful and caring. This man was my husband. He hated the soot and dirt that was a part of his job, but he worked for his family.

Our house was painted brown and was entered off a dirt road. There was a rock wall in front of the porch. You entered directly into what we called the front room. There was a pot belly stove for heat. I cooked on a coal burning stove in the kitchen. There was a water pump above the sink which supplied the best cool, clean well water. The water temperature was 33 degrees at all times which gave us a cool refreshing drink. There was a large tin tub kept in the kitchen for baths. I heated water on the stove to fill the tub. My children loved playing in the water at bath time. The outhouse contained a large Sears and Roebuck catalogue that was used page by page for toilet paper. We had learned that nothing was wasted

Nathaniel had a place where he met up with the other men in the area. They called it the plank. The men put together some barrels and covered them with a large board to make seating for themselves. After dinner many of the young men would tell their wives that they were going to the "plank". This was an all-male gathering place where men could tell jokes, laugh and talk about the issues of the day. They could smoke and drink together and have man talk without worrying about the women. Nathaniel and his friends went to the plank because it was a place that provided the men an outlet from the hard work and drudgery of their lives.

I became comfortable with my life. I hated the lack of social activity in Glen Alum, but truthfully, the yard was a beautiful area with grass for my children to play. Rose bushes, holly hocks and sun flowers surrounded the grass. We had a large area around the back of our house that included a hog pen and a creek. We had a garden that supplied fresh vegetables to cook. Nathaniel planted corn, cabbage, green beans, tomatoes and onions in the garden, so we ate a healthy diet of meat and fresh vegetables. Nathaniel begged me to come outside and watch him garden.

He would say, "Sweets, you don't have to weed, water or do anything other than sit outside with me."

I never went outside until the harvest. Then, I was the first person picking vegetables and loving the fresh produce.

In the late 1930's before WWII a depression was taking place in the United States, but we did not feel the effects of it because we grew our own food. Papa Stuart had a male and female hog and raised pigs. He would kill a hog every winter. Papa had a smoke house where he stored the meat until it was needed. He provided meat to all the family members. So, when Nathaniel won a pig at the company raffle, he knew how to raise it. We had a hog pen and used it for the first time. He also won a calf, but decided not to raise it, and sold it. He was very lucky at the raffles. Mama Marie and Mama Cathy both canned food for the winter. They shared the canned food with me, so I never had to can anything. They provided good food for all our families all winter. There were poor people who worked every day, who did not plant gardens or know how to manage their money and lived in poverty. I was so proud of my husband because he knew how to save money and how to grow our food and I appreciated my mother and mother-in-law who were two smart women and knew how to can our food, make clothing, and preserve meat. We were blessed that we never experienced poverty or hunger.

Nathaniel saved money and bought a dry-cleaning machine and wanted to set up business in our home. He ordered the device from a magazine, so he was dismayed when it arrived, and it was so heavy and large that it took eight men to carry it up the hill to our house. And to our dismay the foundation of the house collapsed when they installed the machine in our home. I wasn't very happy because the dry-cleaning business took over our child's bedroom. Nathaniel and his assistant Thaddeus worked every minute they were not in the mines; cleaning and pressing and delivering clothes. Eventually, Nathaniel had all the customers and the company cleaners was out of business. The company contacted him and he was told to move the business out of the house. He was directed to rent space from the company retail area or he would have to close his business. The retail space rent was too high for a profit, so the eight men had to drag the machine back down the hill, so Nathaniel could return it. He was able to get a refund on some of his costs. I was happy to get my house back.

Nathaniel always felt that the workers the company suspected were saving money were moved to areas of the mine where it was more difficult to dig and slowed down their progress because the workers were paid by the pound of coal they produced. There were workers who spent all of their money with the company who were rewarded with easier digging areas. Nathaniel was actually pulled from a huge productive vein of coal and put deeper in where he must crawl on his knees to get to the coal. It was back breaking work to meet the bare minimum of his quota. Even with these limitations we saved money for our future. Nathaniel explained how he felt the system made it almost impossible for a coal miner to get ahead. He reminded me of the fact that the company owned everything. Our home was rented from the Company. The grocery, liquor store, cleaners, theater and furniture store were owned by the company. When the workers were paid the company knew every penny they spent, where they spent it and could calculate if they saved any money.

CHAPTER

7

Aunt Cynthia and Uncle Robert were my role models for a happy marriage. Aunt Cynthia was tall, slender, and very pretty with a creamy complexion. (her daughter Arlean resembled her as a young adult.) Uncle Robert was built like a football player. He had a dark-brown complexion and very muscular and strong. They were so much in love and had been in love since they met years ago in Virginia when they were young. They had nine children, May Hester the oldest daughter who was at least five or more years older than me; Wesley (we called him little Wesley) was near my age; Louise who was a year younger than me and my constant companion, Herbert; Rudolph their third son died in infancy; Charles, Douglas, Arlean and the baby girl, Geraldine. I loved visiting their house because there was always a baby to hold and love. Uncle Robert loved Cynthia unconditionally. They were one big happy, loving family.

Whenever my cousins came over to visit, I always wanted to go home with them and never wanted them to leave. Mama Carson would tell me that Aunt Cynthia has a large family and does not need to have me added to the bunch. Aunt Cynthia would always support me and ask her to please let Diamond go home with them. I was an only child and wanted to be with other children and loved Aunt Cynthia for her kindness.

Needless to say, I loved going to visit with Aunt Cynthia's family and playing with my cousins. Louise was about a year younger than me and loved to go everywhere with me. We were typical mischievous children who did somethings we were told not to do. We ranged in age from twelve down to infancy. There were fireplaces in most of the rooms of their house for heat. We rolled paper into pretend cigarettes and would light them by sticking the paper into the fireplace and then pretend to smoke the paper. This was Louise's favorite game. She seemed to be drawn to fire and loved to play with it.

I remember, on this particular day, we were all playing in a room with the door closed. We were playing hide and seek. May Hester was "it" and had her eyes closed sitting in the middle of the room counting to one hundred. We ran around the room looking for a hiding place behind the over-stuffed couches and chairs. Louise wore a dress made of a light flannel material. She looked around for a hiding place, but suddenly reached to get something from the mantel over the fireplace and a flame leapt out and caught her dress on fire. We looked on in horrified silence before we could process what was happening before our eyes. Then, we all became hysterical and cried and screamed that Louise was on fire. The adults heard us and tried to open the door. They could not open the door. It had jammed when they tried to push it open. It probably was only minutes, but it seemed like forever before they entered the room. We watched with shocked horror as Louise was enveloped in flames and burned in front of our eyes, and sadly we did not know how to stop the flames. Uncle Robert rushed into the room and threw a blanket over Louise and rolled her on the floor to stop the flames. Louise never recovered. She was gone forever. We were inconsolable. I cried for days and could not sleep alone. This was a horror that took place during my seventh year of life that has left its mark on me for the rest of my days.

As much as I loved my cousins, it took many months before I was comfortable playing at their house. We all had suffered trauma and needed time to heal before we could feel happiness again.

Over eleven years later I was married and had my first son, Wilbert, who was two months old when I went to visit Mama Carson in Rolfe. Aunt Cynthia who lived nearby had a new born baby girl, Geraldine. Aunt Cynthia was in her forties at the time had a very sickly pregnancy. The baby was born prematurely and very pale and weak. Aunt Cynthia came to visit me at Mama Carson's house and told me she was so glad that I was there because she needed me to help her. She tearfully explained that her baby was not thriving and was slowly fading away, and that she believed that the baby wasn't getting enough to eat. She felt that her illness during the pregnancy had affected her ability to produce milk in her breast to feed the baby. The doctor gave her a formula for the baby, but the baby's mouth was very small, and she was so weak that she could not suckle the hard nipple on the baby bottle. Aunt Cynthia asked me if I would share some of my breast milk with her baby. I was honored to help Aunt Cynthia. I told her that I had enough milk and that I could feed both babies while I was there. I wanted to do anything I could to save Geraldine's life. We set up a plan for me to come to her house at the same time every day and breast feed her baby. I nursed Geraldine every day for the week that I was there and when the day arrived that I had to return to my home, Geraldine was thriving and strong enough to nurse from the baby bottle. I was grateful to God that I was able to be helpful to my Aunt Cynthia and baby, Geraldine.

Uncle Robert attended the apostolic church and often invited Consuela and me to his church for special services. I was a young mother and wanted to be baptized but had never been baptized because I feared getting water in my nose. Many years prior Mama Carson asked me why I wasn't baptized, and I told her of my fear and she told me that when the time came for my baptism to hold my nose and I would be fine. On this particular evening Consuela and I went to church with Uncle Robert to attend a revival service. I was caught up in the singing and preaching and before I knew it I was at the altar feeling the spirit of God. The pastor of the church who had known me since I was a baby asked me if I wanted to be baptized and I said, "Yes".

To my surprise they told me that I would be baptized that evening and the deacons began to fill the baptismal pool immediately and the ladies of the church took me aside and prepared me for baptism. Before I had time to think, I was in the pool with the pastor ready for my baptism. I remembered Mama Carson's words and put one hand on my nose to squeeze it shut. The pastor immediately removed my hand from my nose. I put it back. He moved my hand away. This went on for several tries until finally the pastor realized that I was determined to hold my nose. He dunked me in the water and I did not know what happened. I felt as if the doors of heaven had opened and I was rising and going straight to heaven. It was a wonderful feeling. Then suddenly someone said to me "say Hallelujah!" and touched me. After I felt that touch the spirit left and I was back to reality. I will never forget that night and that feeling. I believed that I would have been filled with the Holy Ghost that evening if the person had not touched me. I was a Methodist visiting a Pentecostal church and did not expect to have such a powerful reaction to baptism. I often wondered what would have happened if I had not been touched. Uncle Robert was a religious man who talked to us about God and holiness and wanted Consuela and I to be saved. We loved him and enjoyed going to church with him although we never became members of his church.

CHAPTER

8

My mother, Marie married again shortly after the birth of my first child. She married Bob Davis, a guitar playing, blues singing old family friend. No one in the family wanted her to marry Bob, but she did. Mama had a mind of her own and made her own decisions. She moved to Welch, West Virginia with Bob. Her marriage to Bob did not keep her from often visiting with us. Bob loved my children and enjoyed having us around.

Uncle Luke married Consuela and moved her in with him, Mama Carson, and Uncle Wesley soon after Nathaniel and I married. When I left Rolfe, Consuela took care of Mama Carson during the day, and over time she and Luke fell in love. We were like sisters and Nathaniel and Luke were like brothers. We visited them often because we had a car. Consuela and Luke had their first baby, Isaac around the same time I had Nate, Jr. Luke worked in the mines near Rolfe. The coal mine was the only employment for people who did not have professional degrees. There was always work for teachers, doctors and other professionals.

CHAPTER

9

I remember not feeling well about a year and a half after Wilbert's birth. I was feeling terrible and went to see the company doctor. This new doctor gave me 3 large pills and told me to take these pills and all my sickness will go away. I showed Mama Carson the pills and told her what the doctor told me. She looked at the pills and told me not to take them. "Throw those pills out", she said, "You are sick because you are carrying another baby. If you take those pills you will kill your baby.' I listened to Mama Carson and did not take the pills and later found out that I was indeed pregnant and had a very healthy pregnancy. I was so blessed to have my grandmother near me and have her advice. I thought about how my life would have changed if I had taken the pills.

My second child, Nathaniel, Jr. was a very easy delivery. No Amazons waiting for me to deliver. The doctor, Mama and Mama Cathy helped me through the delivery. Nathaniel, Jr was a healthy, eight pounds chocolate baby boy with thick, black curly hair. My husband told me he had prayed that his boys would have beautiful hair because the girls in his family had beautiful hair and the boys were left out. He said, "Girls can go to the beauty shop". His prayers were answered because both our boys had beautiful baby hair.

Papa Stuart had a special affection for my second born son, Nate, Jr. About a year after his birth, he began stopping by to see the baby on his way home from the mines. When he arrived, he would look inside his lunch box and find something to give the baby to eat. I loved my father-in-law but was not happy that he gave my baby stale food that had been sitting in his lunch box all day while he worked in the coal mines. However, I knew it was out of love for my baby, and that he saved my baby something special. Nate, Jr. loved it and smiled waving his fat little arms around in excitement and gobbled up whatever morsel of food my father-in-law stuffed into his mouth. I never said anything about my fears and let him hold and feed the baby. When he left, I asked God to please protect my baby from any illness that could come from stale food. The food did not hurt him; he is one of my healthiest children.

One day, Papa came to visit and asked that I bring Nate, Jr. to him for a blessing. All my children were home, so I asked Papa to please bless all of my children, and he said, "I pray for all my grandchildren, but I have a special blessing for Nate." I brought Nate to him and he anointed him, laid hands on him and prayed. Papa gave him his special blessing. I was happy for Nate.

It was nice having all the family living near. I could visit with the ladies and our children would play together. I dressed Wilbert and Nathaniel Jr. in the morning and we would go visit Mama Cathy in the big house. I would chat with the women of the family, and all the cousins would play together. The cousins were all boys, Paul, (Jane's son), Albert, Jr and Clarence., (Lillian's sons). Wilbert II, and Nathaniel, Jr. would play happily with their cousins for a while and then one of the other boys would tell me that my son, Wilbert beat up one of the kids. "Diamond, Wilbert hit me with his fist" one would say. I would always chastise Wilbert by spanking him and we would go home. Now, I wonder if they were all fighting and then blamed Wilbert when things did not go their way. Nate, Jr was the "baby" so he was too young to be in the fray. Mama Cathy told me that Nathaniel, Sr. was a fighter when he was a young boy, so I did not know what to believe.

CHAPTER 10

Two years after Nathaniel, Jr. (Teddy) was born I finally had a daughter on a beautiful, sunny April day. The doors were open, and the weather was great. Mama came to assist as always, but this time she wanted me to hurry and have the baby because she had a trip planned for early May. Her church had an assembly in Nashville, Tennessee and she did not want to miss it. She told me, "You better hurry up and have this baby. I am going to the Assembly." I said, "You are going to leave me for the assembly?" I felt so hurt. I wasn't involved in her church in those days. I felt hurt because she was putting her meeting ahead of me and my baby. She pressured me to have the baby soon. Lucky for me the baby came the last week in April. After my daughter was born Mama stayed with me for one week and left me in bed. She usually gave me two weeks to get on my feet and take over for myself. Just so happened, Consuela, Luke's wife was visiting from Rolfe and came to help me for the second week. She told Marie she could leave and that she would stay and take care of me.

Consuela stayed until I was on my feet. I had no problems with my third delivery and had a fat, healthy, 8lb, 6oz, baby girl with a creamy complexion and a little brown hair but mostly bald, that was the love of my life. I had my girl and I named her Arlene. I thought Arlene was a pretty doll, but Nathaniel teased me because she was nearly bald and had a very serious expression. Nathaniel loved my little Arlene and would be wrapped around her little finger for life.

CHAPTER

During the Fall of 1942 there was a constant downpouring of rain and high winds which covered Glen Alum for many days. The skies were dark and menacing when the men went to the mines daily, but all the families had to hunker down at night and wait and pray for the heavy rain and howling wind to end.

We were awakened early in the morning after we were finally able to sleep by unusually loud noises coming from the wind and rain, and then a huge crash and dragging sound. Nathaniel jumped up to go investigate the noises. By the time he reached our front door, his youngest sister Lillian and her family were rushing to our porch. She shouted that their house was falling down the hill and that they had barely escaped before the house started rolling down the hill. Lillian said she felt the house rocking back and forth and awakened the family and they had to run for their lives. We embraced her family and made them comfortable. Nate and her husband Albert went out to investigate.

In the daylight, we found out that a mudslide had dislodged the stilts holding the front end of their house and washed it away from its foundation. We were so relieved that no one was hurt. The children were traumatized but with soothing and love they were able to sleep through the next night. Our house was on level ground, so they felt safe with us. Eventually, they found other lodging for themselves, and were able to move forward with their lives.

CHAPTER

12

Glen Alum was so far up in the mountains it did not show on the map, but World War II came to Glen Alum. In 1942 the draft board was formed, and they began to draft young men from our area for World War II. My husband, Nathaniel was drafted shortly after Arlene's birth. However, he was a new father and had two other small children he was given an exemption. Matthew Lawrence (ML) the second from the youngest brother was drafted and spent his entire enlisted time on the front lines. He served under General Patton. He was in the middle of the hot battles but was never harmed. He spoke of dead bodies falling around him. He felt it was a miracle he was able to survive. He stayed on the front line until the day the war was over. He was not allowed to return home for Mama Cathy's funeral. He loved his mother dearly and not attending her funeral hurt him to his heart.

He saved a fellow soldier by carrying him to safety on his back but could not understand why he survived. He received three medals for his military service. Although, he survived the war, his life was ruined. He aged about 20 years during the four years he fought, and his hair was pure white when he returned home. He was 25, second youngest son, but looked like the oldest. He became an alcoholic and never married. He did not father any children. Nathaniel told me not to be hard on ML because of his alcoholism. He said that ML has seen things no man should see, and the alcohol gave him some relief from his horrible memories. We loved ML and forgave him for any inadequacies, because the war had sucked out his youth and his spirit. What was left was only a shell of the man he had been, and we mourned for that man.

In his later year's he hocked his medals for liquor and I often wondered what sort of person would buy someone's medals and pretend they won them. M.L. talked very little about the war, but I often imagined some stranger wearing M.L.'s medals and telling tall tales about the war.

The baby boy, Thomas Lee was also drafted and served until an injury sent him home. After his return, Thomas married Betty and they had ten children. Bernice's son, Junior Pool was drafted into the Navy and served his time on a ship until the war was over. He was the cook for the captain. They did not allow black men on the ships to fight. However, Junior survived many attacks and completed his service. Little Wesley (Cynthia & Robert's son) also served in the Navy during WWII and became a career sailor and retired honorably from military service. The men in our family served our country well during WWII and other wars.

CHAPTER 13

Work slowed down at the coal mines around 1943. They don't lay-off, like they do in the auto plants in the North, but the work slows down. Nathaniel was down to one or two days a week. When the mine began to dry up industrious people who wanted to improve themselves would move on. You can't live on the paycheck for working one day a week. Most of the men started looking for other coal mines to find work. Everyone knew that eventually there would be no coal in the mine.

I suggested to Nathaniel that since he was not working full time, that it is a good time to visit Luke in Rolfe and see if he knew of any work there. Nathaniel agreed and the next weekend we drove to Rolfe and stayed a week with Luke and Consuela while Nathaniel looked for work. Luke told Nathaniel he probably could get a job at Rolfe with him, and there were several other mines in the vicinity. Nathaniel applied but wasn't hired at Rolfe, so he applied at several other locations and eventually he was hired in Coalton,

West Virginia not far from Rolfe. Then Luke decided he would apply for Coalton and he was hired also. We ended up with houses across the road from each other.

Moving to Coalton from Glen Alum in 1942 was like moving from a Manhattan Brownstone to a Bronx tenement in the 80's. Nathaniel was grateful for the work, but the housing was horrible. When we drove there it was Fall, cold air and dust seemed to block out the sun. This place looked poor. Many of the people looked weathered, both black and white. We were assigned a yellow house with white trim that was dirty and looked dingy, both inside and out. The children's room was partially furnished with a small bed. We kept the bed for our boys.

The next morning, I awoke to my boys crying and screaming in pain. They were covered in insect bites and were miserable. They looked like they had been eaten alive. The bedroom was infested with bedbugs. We had to get rid of the bed and mattress by burning them. My Sister-in-law, Lillian came to help me. She advised me to boil water until it was scalding hot, then add a disinfectant and pour it over the floor, in the corners and in any cracks where bugs could hide. After several days of the scalding hot water treatment, we bought a new bed for the boys and allowed them to sleep in their room. It took us over a week to clean the place and make it habitable.

The conditions in Coalton were horrible but we were able to make this a very happy time in our lives. We had Luke and Consuela nearby and this was a joy. We had a backyard and Nathaniel planted a garden as always. Luke and Consuela didn't have much back yard because a stream ran across the back of their house which gave it charm.

Nature is always beautiful. It was so much fun living near our best friends. Nathaniel and Luke enjoyed working together, and I enjoyed visiting with Consuela and their children. They had a son, Isaac who was the same age as Nate, Jr. and a daughter, Margarite, who was two months older than Arlene. We found joy in the small things.

In Glen Alum we lived farthest away from the stack of the coal mine. We did not get blow back from the coal dust. We lived near the stack in the Coalton coal mines. We breathed the coal dust and felt the grim daily.

After we lived in Coalton a few months Nathaniel took a flu like illness in his lungs and had to go to the hospital. While he was there recuperating he had time to think about his life and our sons and what kind of life he wanted for us. He told me he was unhappy and never planned on working in the mines forever and that he wanted to get away soon. He said he was thankful that he had a job and could take care of his family, but that it was hard back breaking work although he had never complained. He did not want his sons to become coal miners and he did not want to die in a coal mine. We were never told the cause or nature of Nate's illness. After a month of hospitalization, they sent him home and said he could go back to work. I suppose they did not know what it was at the time. It is well known today that black lung disease is a major killer of coal miners.

CHAPTER 14

I n the mean-time Katy Mae, Nathaniel's niece was living in the Capitol, Charleston, West Virginia. She and I corresponded often because we were the same age and had a lot in common. Katy wrote that she met a nice young man, Freddie Maxwell, who was working in Charleston, and had moved there from Chicago. Later, she wrote that Freddy had fallen in love with her and she loved him more than she could have imagined. She, also, shared their plans to marry soon. In the next letter Katy wrote that they were married, and they may move to Chicago and live there. When I wrote back I told her that if she moved to Chicago to please let me know because Nathaniel and I wanted to move away from the coal mines. She answered that "If Freddie takes me to Chicago I will let you know." A month later I received another letter "Diamond, we are moving to Chicago" Katy wrote. I was so excited. Although we had lived in Coalton for only six months we wanted to get away from the coal mines. When I received a letter from Katy confirming that she was doing well in Chicago and that they had an apartment. I wondered if we moved there could we get jobs soon after? She wrote that jobs were plentiful, and we were welcome to stay with them until we found work. I told Nathaniel "Katy Mae is in Chicago and she said we could come at any time." I told him that she said that we did not need to worry about a job, because jobs are plentiful. She shared that there may be a problem getting a place to live that will accept kids. I wrote her that my kids are so nice, that I wasn't worried about finding a place to live. So, I asked Nathaniel if he was serious about moving and if he wanted to go to Chicago and he agreed that he wanted to move. I wrote back and told Kate that we planned to come to Chicago very soon. Then we had the task of telling Consuela and Luke that we were moving. They were so sad. "Don't leave us" they said. We told them that if things worked out they could come, also.

Then our parents got involved. They were furious and said, "You left Glenn Alum, moved to Coalton and now you want to go to Chicago. When are you going to settle down and be satisfied"? They were the voices of doom. They told us that we would change and become bad people. They thought we would separate. We would not respect our marriage vows and would have affairs, because that was how the people who lived in the big cities behaved. They believed that we would be corrupted, and they thought we were crazy. We listened, but we were going anyway. "What are you going to do with your children", they asked "Are you going to run off and leave your children". Nate said, "I am going for my children. I do not want my boys going into the coal mines".

We women always need to make the plans. So, I thought of a plan that would make sure our children were safe until we could bring them to live with us. I told Nathaniel that we could leave the boys with Aunt Jean and Uncle Buddy and that we could leave our baby girl who was only ten months old with Mama. Mama and Bob loved our baby girl and would take good care of her. Aunt Jean & Uncle Buddy agreed to take the boys.

These were the most difficult decisions I had made in my entire life. The weight of choosing to leave my beautiful innocent babies behind was heavy on my heart. I knew that Mama had to face the same decisions when she allowed me to live in Rolfe with Mama Carson when I was seven years old to start my education. It was the best solution for me, but it left her out of my early years. Now I know how she felt leaving me behind. I had to choose what was best for my babies and not what would make me happy.

Nathaniel and I had discussed our choices and after much heart rendering and serious discussions we both felt that we should go on this journey together for the sake of our marriage, and I truly believed that we would be separated from our children no more than one month. That would give us time to get jobs and find an apartment that would accept children. We were not familiar with housing restrictions, other than the separation of black and white people. I must confess that if my family had not been supportive and loving to my children, I would not have been able to leave them.

We decided not to tell the children that we would be moving. We told the boys that we were going on a short trip and that we would be back to take them home very soon. They were not disturbed when we dropped them off because they had slept over at their Aunt's house on occasion. There was no way we could make my leaving easy for my baby. We had never been separated. Our baby girl held out her arms and said "Ma Ma" as she watched us leave. She wanted to leave with us. I hugged and kissed her one more time and told her "Mama will be back". My heart broke and tears welled in my eyes as we continued out the door.

That was saddest day of our lives, when we had to leave our children. We cried as we drove away, but we had to go. It was for our children's future. Our hearts were bleeding because we had to leave the children to make life better for them. We left crying, driving and promising each other that we would send for them as soon as we moved into our own apartment. Nathaniel said it is enough that he had to work in dirt and grime and breath foul air, but he wanted a better place for our children. We had to secure jobs and a safe place to raise our children and could not drag them into the uncertainty that we felt. This may be our only opportunity to get them away from the coal mines. We felt that both of us working would make our plan move faster.

CHAPTER

15

Katy Mae, tall, attractive with thick dark eyebrows and slender and Freddy, tall, slender with a dark complexion was jovial, and full of wisdom lived in a nice apartment building on Michigan Ave. It was a three-story brick, building and their two-bedroom apartment was on the third floor. We had our own private bedroom that was very comfortable. Freddy had his own business selling medicine and herbs, so Katy Mae never had to work. Freddy knew all the herbal remedies that had been passed down through the generations that could heal most ailments. People believed in him and his remedies and paid for his medicine and his consultations. He was a good provider and they lived a good life. We enjoyed living with them, but we needed to find a place that would accept children. We could not rest and never lost sight of our goal.

After moving to Chicago "pop" we both got jobs as soon as we got there. We had never been in a big city in our lives. Katy Mae got the newspaper and told me all the details on how to find an ad for a job in the "Want Ads" and how to get the streetcar to the businesses, but we went alone. I got a job in a hat factory, and Nathaniel got a job painting tanks for the government.

Nathaniel was so accustomed to hard work that he could spray paint a tank without any effort, so the other guys hated him. They called him that "country boy" who is up here working like a slave. He was a source of irritation for the other workers. He continued to work hard because that was all he knew, and it did help him receive many pay bonuses. The other workers were held to a standard set by the amount of work he did. He spray-painted tanks and it was so easy in comparison to what he knew. The work he did there was like a vacation after digging coal out of the hard ground and then manually loading it on a train car. They brought him a car load of tanks and he would have them all spray painted before lunch time. The other men thought he was working them to death. He spray-painted tanks and I made hats.

A worker brought me a big box of hats that had no form and I had a form in front of me that I placed it on and then put the hat in a box for the next person. We made ladies hats. The girls that worked on the steam irons had to stand all day and were hot and uncomfortable because they steamed the hats before they came to me. After the hats were steamed they would take the shape of the form where I placed them. The girls grumbled because new girls usually started on the steaming job and then worked up to the comfortable job of sitting in a chair and placing the hat on the form. "How did she get that job" and "She just walked in the building," they complained. I believe God was looking out for me and I was blessed. They were mad at me and wanted me to work on the steam table. My employer was happy with the work I did.

I tired of all the animosity and found a better paying job at the International Restaurant where I was hired as a bus girl. Work was great in Chicago and we saved our money to purchase a home, so our children could come and be with us. Unfortunately, Katy Mae was correct it was virtually impossible to find a place that would accept children to rent. We were still living with Katy Mae and Freddie Maxwell because we could not find a place big enough for our family that would accept children as residents, and we would not accept a place that would not accept our children. We knew we could not live in Chicago forever.

This is how our move to Vancouver became a reality. Bernice, Nathaniel's sister had a friend, Gary who was on his way to Vancouver, Washington to work. He told Nathaniel that there were good paying jobs in Vancouver and that he would be building ships for the government for great wages. Nathaniel told him that because of his family, he needed him to write and let us know if there would be houses for families because we wanted to bring our children with us. He said he would write and it was not long before a letter came to Bernice from Gary that said, "Tell Nathaniel he will have everything he wanted". There were houses and plenty of jobs, and that not only could Nathaniel get a job but that I could get a job. He wrote that there were good schools for the children and that Vancouver is a beautiful place to live.

We had lived in Chicago for eight months, but Vancouver was our dream. Our goal was to get a place for our children. A place where we could work and have a decent home and schools to educate our children. Nathaniel and I talked, and he told me that he would go and then send for me and the kids, but as I thought about it I decided that I was going with him. I told Katy and Freddy about Nathaniel's plan to go to Vancouver without me and that I wanted to go with him. I believed we needed to be together for the sake of our marriage and our children. Freddy told me "Little Bit, if you want to go with Nathaniel you should tell him". I told him that I wanted to go with him and he said "you can go. I thought you wanted to go get the kids", and I asked if it would be ok to give the money to Mama and have her bring the kids? He said that was a good plan, and he told me to get ready we would be leaving soon.

Once again, we were planning to move on. I told my boss at the International Restaurant that I was leaving. She asked me why I had to go? I told her my husband was moving on to look for better living conditions where we could raise our children. She asked if I would let him go alone. "You are such a smart girl", she said and "I have great plans for you". I could not believe she was crying and asked me to stay. She told me "Diamond if you ever come back to Chicago you have a job".

In those days, we could deposit money in the post office for safekeeping. When we arrived in Chicago we sold our car and saved that money and we were saving money every week at the Post Office from our jobs. We had more than enough money to get the train tickets to Vancouver for us, Mama, and the children. I went to the Post Office and drew out all our money and bought train tickets to Vancouver, so we could leave the next day.

A SHIPBUILDING TRADITION

The Kaiser Shipyard followed a tradition started near this site as early as the rnid- 1800s with shipbuilding activity at Fort Vancouver.

All escort carrier slides info the Columbiu WI its way to fight World War II.

The city's earliest war boom came when the United States entered World War I in 1917. In a yard just down- stream from the Interstate Bridge, the Standifer Company built ships for the federal government. That yard was hailed as the only yard in the world

Kaiser's World War II Vancouver Shipyard was on the site now occupied by a business park just downstream from this tower. This wartime emergency yard was established in January 1942, a inonth after the Japanese had attacked Pearl Harbor. The yard quicklv expanded to 12

ACOM-UNITY EXPLODES

As the pleasant and sunny Sunday of December 7, 1941, dawned, Vancouver was a peaceful community of 18,009 people.

The Japanese attack on Pearl Harbor and the subsequent declaration of war. by the United States changed all that. Within months, an influx of people recruited from around the nation for the Kaiser

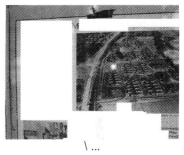

\ ...

Hudson House, a wartime 110 using project built east of the shipyard, housed hundreds of workers. It was struck by fire on Nov. 13, leaving seven dead and 16 injure«.

Shipyard tripled the city's population to jam more than 100,000 people into the greater Vancouver area.

To meet the sudden demand, the Vancouver Housing Authority (VHA) formed, holding its first meeting February 7, 1942. Within 18 months the local agency, financed by the federal government, had acquired 1,600 acres and started six new communities in and around the city.

Within rnonths, the wartime housing of McLoughlin Heights, Ogden Meadows, Fruit Valley, Bagley Downs, Burton Homes and Plain

CHAPTER

16

I t took us three days on the train to reach Vancouver. It was a long, boring train ride. Much of the scenery was similar to West Virginia. Nathaniel was so glad I came with him for companionship. The grandeur of our vast country passed before our eyes, but we were so anxious that we did not appreciate the spectacle of nature. The train rocked, hummed and passed through long black tunnels and around the mountains on narrow ledges that were wide enough for only the train tracks. While looking out the window it appeared that the train would fall off the side of the mountains. Luckily, we are from West Virginia, so every day we drove around ridges on roads going thru and around the mountains without any barriers between the cars and the drop-off. I was one of the few women in our community that could drive a car.

To help pass the time we played a game that required us to describe what our lives would be like in Vancouver. We described where we would live and how many bedrooms we would have for our children. Sadly, we did not know what to expect and would run out of imagination very quickly. We had put our trust in the word of a friend and prayed that we would not be disappointed. This move was so important to our family's survival that we could not think about failing. We weren't able to sleep.

I felt like African-American pioneers moving west. This was a great adventure for us going on faith to a place in the Great North West where I had never visited and only read about in my geography classes. I had become a part of the Great Migration of our people from the South seeking a better life.

Along with us, the train was full of young soldiers going to a fort in Washington before being shipped overseas. They looked so young and afraid. I was 24 years old, married with three children and feeling very grownup when I looked at their young faces. I prayed that God would keep them safe and end the war soon for all of our sakes.

I thought about my brother-in-law, M.L. who had been drafted into the war. Did he ride on a train like this one not knowing what to expect, or what would be his final-destination? Was he frightened and alone like these young soldiers? I hoped he made a friend, so he could talk to someone and share his feelings.

Nathaniel and I talked about our families and how we would invite them to join us if Vancouver lived up to our expectations. We were a tight knit family and wanted to share everything together. Soon, we heard the conductor shout, "Vancouver, Washington is the next station."

CHAPTER

17

The day we arrived in Vancouver we applied for jobs and signed up for housing. Nathaniel was hired to become a welder and I was hired on the maintenance staff. I could have become a welder also, but because of my small statue I did not feel confident that I could handle wearing the heavy vest and mask worn for safety, so I was content to work in maintenance.

We were assigned a very nice house in the McLaughlin Heights, area of Vancouver, Washington. While I was there at the housing authority, I told them that my mother was coming to Vancouver to bring our children. I explained that she would apply for a job and asked if they would assign the house directly behind our home to my mother, so she could help babysit our children when they arrived. They agreed and saved the house for Mama. I was delighted because our lives were finally moving in the direction we had prayed for.

We went home and wrote a letter to mama and the children. We shared our good fortune with them and enclosed the train-fare, so they could join us immediately.

We walked around our new neighborhood to explore. It was magnificent! Everything looked new and fresh. There was an elementary school nearby for our oldest boy. Everything we had been told about Vancouver was true. After Coalton, this was wonderful. Our home had new appliances. We had an electric stove and a refrigerator. There was a place for a washing machine inside the house, so this would be my first purchase. It was all amazing to us. There were fields of grass and wild flowers surrounding the housing units. It was beautiful to us and we talked about our bright future until we fell asleep. We slept two days.

My maintenance job required that I crawl through a hole in a large pitch-black tank with a small brush and a helmet that had a light to help me see. I cleaned the weld made by the welders with my brush and made sure there was no debris from small fragments left on the weld across the tank. Nathaniel took to welding with his usual hard working and perfectionist attitude and learned quickly. It wasn't long before he was asked to teach others how to weld.

Mama was ready to join us immediately and did not mind leaving her husband, Bob behind. She bought train tickets with the money for herself and our three kids. She was able to get two sleeping car berths to accommodate the four of them. She told me how the train's sleeping car porters were so kind and helpful. They made sure she had a table in the dining car for herself and the children. They understood that travelling with three small children was a difficult task. They helped her get the boys in bed every night. The children loved looking out the window from the sleeping car and watching the night lights go by. They were soon asleep. She was grateful for the kindness of the sleeping care porters. It was a long train ride from West Virginia to Washington State.

It was the best feeling I have ever felt when I saw Mama and our children get off the train in Vancouver. We arrived at the station two hours early because we could not wait for their arrival time. Our dream was complete. Tears of joy were flowing, and we could not get enough hugs and kisses. We felt so blest to have our family together once again. God was so good to us. We had well-paying jobs and a nice home to raise our family. We were finally reunited with our children, so life could not get any better.

Mama got a job immediately and moved into her house. Her husband, Bob joined her soon after. There was work for everyone, so we wrote Luke and Consuela and told Nathaniel's family as well. Soon the Amazons and most of our extended family had migrated to Vancouver, Washington.

McLoughlin Heights was an area with newer homes and a very beautiful location overlooking the bay. Everyone wanted to live there. There were other areas that were older and not quite as scenic that also offered housing for shipyard workers. One was called Bagley Downs. Many of our relatives were not happy when the Housing Authority began sending them to the Bagley Down neighborhood for housing. They grumbled behind my back that "Diamond was able to get her mother into McLoughlin Heights why not us". I guess it is impossible to make everyone happy. We were so thankful and joyous for our kids and Mama bringing them to join us that nothing anyone said could bring us down.

CHAPTER

18

One of our goals when we moved to Vancouver was to work as much as we physically could and save as much money as possible. We knew that our jobs were temporary and would end whenever the war ended. Nathaniel reminded me that our jobs were a part of the war effort and could end without notice. We had a plan that Nathaniel would pay all the household bills and save half of his check, and I would pick up small expenses and save as much as I could from my check. My only splurge was my May Tag washing machine. It became my pride and joy. Nate worked days and I tried to work afternoons so I could be home with our children during the day. Mama would try to work day-shift, so she could be my back up.

Whenever we had the time the family would go to a movie or we would take the children to Jansen Beach amusement park. We took the children to the neighborhood park every Sunday after church services. We were lucky to find a minister holding church services in his living room.

We met some great people and made friends with many families like ours.

Most of the people we met were from the deep South; places like Mississippi and Alabama. For the most part, we met good hard-working people who wanted to improve their lives. My oldest child attended integrated schools and there were no problems at the school that made him feel uncomfortable. This was my first experience living with integration.

CHAPTER

19

The shipyard crews were integrated, so blacks and whites had the same jobs on the same crew. This took some adjustment for many of the white Southern girls. Although there was Jim Crow in West Virginia, it was not as overt as in the "deep" South. When we were hired the Managers talked to us and told us that the Government did not allow any discrimination and that the rules would be enforced.

Most of the crew members minded their own business and did not bother other crew members. We got along well until a white woman from Texas joined our crew. She told N-word jokes during our break time and laughed loudly to our faces. Although she would be the only one laughing, she continued to insult us during our break time with these racist jokes. It had gotten to the point that I dreaded break time because of this woman's crude, mean jokes. One afternoon before my shift I asked to see the manager and was admitted into his office. I explained to him how this woman was insulting us with racist jokes during our break time. He told me he would handle the situation. He called her in and told her that there would be no more jokes of any kind during our break time, or she would be fired. Afterwards, she stopped telling jokes, and we were able to work together peacefully.

One of my proudest days at the shipyard was when they launched the aircraft carrier we helped to build. There was a ceremony and all the workers and very important officials from Vancouver and the Navy brass were invited. I will never forget seeing the huge vessel sliding gracefully into the water. It was a source of pride that my husband and I had a small part in the assembly of that great vessel that would be used to keep our country safe. I prayed that it would help end the war and bring ML and all the soldiers home soon.

Once again, the long arm of the draft board from West Virginia sent a letter to Nathaniel in Vancouver in 1944 asking him to report for the draft. At that time we had three small children and a new baby on the way. Nathaniel was working to support the war effort so once again he was allowed an exemption. He was their best welder, and he trained the new hires. We felt we were doing our part for the war. They had M.L. and Thomas which was enough sacrifice from the Stuart family. I did not want to lose my husband and become a war widow.

Nathaniel bought a car and used it to make more money for our family. He became a jitney driver to allow the car to pay for itself. Jitney drivers are people who used their own cars to take other people to places for a fee. They would be similar to the Uber drivers of today, but all the drivers were independent; there was no company involvement. People called, and Nathaniel would take them to their destination and they would call later or prearrange when he would pick them up. He drove the jitney whenever he was not working at the shipyards. Nathaniel worked all the time and told me he wanted to make as much money as possible, so we could go to Detroit and get really-good, permanent jobs making automobiles.

CHAPTER 20

I found out that I was pregnant shortly after we arrived in Vancouver. I wasn't surprised because after the three-day train ride to Vancouver, we stayed in bed over twenty-four hours because we were exhausted. We had to adjust to the time change. I surmised that I conceived during that time. This was around August 1943. I was able to work every day until my 6th month. Then, I came home and took care of my three children and waited for the new baby. My next- door neighbor was suffering with cancer and too ill to work. She stayed home to care for her children. We shared looking out for the children while they played out doors. We became lasting friends.

For the first time, I had regular pre-natal care and would give birth in a hospital. We had a very forward-thinking Doctor who counselled my husband and I about child birth after my regular checkups. The Doctor projected the birth for May 3rd, but the baby was very late and was not born until May 20.

I went into labor in the early hours of May 20th around 1:00 am in the morning. When my husband and mother who were exhausted arrived home after working their afternoon shift jobs at the shipyards, I told them that I was in labor and needed to go to the hospital. They told me to get dressed and called an ambulance to take me to the hospital. When the ambulance arrived, I asked who was going with me, and they told me they were tired and put me in the ambulance and sent me to the hospital alone. I had a difficult time with this birth because the baby was so large that the doctor had to do some repair work and I was told I had to stay in the hospital for ten days. I gave birth to a 9 pounds 8oz, beautiful, healthy, baby boy with smooth dark brown skin and whose head was covered with silky black hair. I named this baby boy, Bryant Vincent. He was a handsome baby boy and the nurses that helped with the delivery were so proud of how big and healthy he was that he became the talk of the hospital.

After the birth, I was put in my room and no one came to visit me. I was all alone and cried all the time. The Doctor noticed my loneliness and asked me, "where is your family?" I told him that Mama and Nate worked afternoons and could not come to the hospital for regular visiting hours. The doctor told me he would let my husband know that they will let him in no matter how late at night. He should just let them know he is my husband. Maybe my husband could have gotten off work, but he did not know how, and he had three young children in his care. There was no family leave in the 1940's. He came to see me when he could. Ten days was a long time away from my other children. I was lonesome and still cried all day. I told the nurse that I wanted to see my children. In those days children were not allowed in hospitals. My doctor told my husband that he could bring the children to my first-floor window, so I could see them. He did and the children and I were so happy to see one another. They missed me as much as I missed them. This was my first hospital experience. I thank God that this birth was in the hospital. This was a complicated birth that could have killed me. I had delivered three children with natural birth and knew something was wrong. I believe my suffering would have been unbearable without the anesthesia.

In June 1944, we took Bryant Vincent home and we became a family of six. The doctor asked Nathaniel and I to come in for family planning counselling. He explained various methods of birth control, and recommended we not have more children. He explained that if we continued to have children that we would probably force ourselves into poverty. It was up to us to make the decision, but he was recommending birth control. We knew of birth control but did not know the methods or how to get the prescriptions. He explained the methods and we decided to take his advice and not have another baby without planning for the birth. Our family was complete with three boys and one girls.

CHAPTER

21

Everything wasn't peaches and cream while we lived in Vancouver. We had some heartbreaking events while living in Vancouver. One afternoon, we took our family for a drive. Nathaniel, and I and our baby boy, Bryant Vincent were in the front seat of the car. The other three children were in the back seat. Teddy our second son was behind the driver's seat, Arlene was in the middle, Wilbert II was behind me. Teddy who was four years old at the time, abruptly opens the door and falls out of the car on the street. Luckily, the other two children were not sucked out of the car with him. We were able to stop the car and move him out of harm's way. We rushed Teddy to the hospital.

His bandaged body looked like the "Mummy" when we brought him home. It was horrifying. His younger sister was frightened by his appearance. He had been bruised, bumped and scraped from head to toe, but no broken bones. He was so fortunate that nothing was broken other than a chipped tooth. He was strong and resilient and recovered quickly.

There wasn't any lasting damage from the accident. We were so thankful.

Our daughter, Arlene became ill with pneumonia and had to be hospitalized at two years old. There is nothing worse than leaving your baby in the hospital over night at that young age. I had to leave her because of the other children could not stay with me. When it was time for me to leave my brave little girl said, "Don't worry Mama, I'm going to be alright." I held back the tears because I did not want to frighten her. She was right. She was able to come home two days later.

There were some special events that made us joyful as well. Mama Marie took Arlene to downtown Vancouver with her on Saturdays by bus. They would stand in front of a photography shop and admire the photographs in the window while waiting for the bus that would carry them home. The owner of the shop approached Mama and asked her if he could photograph Arlene. He wanted to put her picture in the window. He offered to give her a free package of photographs if she would consent. He said that he wanted everyone to feel welcome at his shop. He hoped that putting Arlene's picture in his shop window would make African-American families feel welcome to come inside his shop.

I agreed, and Mama took Arlene to the shop the following weekend for her photography session. He did beautiful work. We still have the eight-by-ten photograph of our two-year-old daughter. It became a source of pride when Mama took Arlene downtown and they could see her picture in the window while they waited for the bus.

CHAPTER

22

I stayed home a year after Bryant Vincent's birth. By the time I was ready to go back to work the shipyard was laying off people. Nathaniel was a top welder and his boss wanted to keep him. Nathaniel told his boss that I needed a job and that he would not be able to stay unless we both could work. His boss found a job for me that was better than the one I had before the baby. I cleaned small tanks and was paid more money. The other women became jealous because there were more large tanks than small. Consequently, some shifts there wasn't anything for me to do. The supervisor would find some busy work for me and I would get paid my regular salary.

We stayed at the shipyard until it closed, and then moved to Rodeo, California to work in the shipyards there. A friend of Nathaniel had found work in Rodeo. He asked Nate to come there and work because they were looking for an expert welder. Unfortunately, this job lasted only eleven months before that shipyard closed as well. We tried and tried to find other jobs but were not successful in finding employment.

Again, we decided that it was time for us to move to a place where jobs were plentiful. We had always dreamed of moving to Detroit and now was our time, to realize that dream. Aunt Jean and Uncle Buddy moved to Detroit many years earlier and offered us a place to stay, whenever we decided to move there. They had purchased a three-story Victorian home and had plenty of room for our family. Luke, Consuela and their children had moved to Detroit when we moved to California. Luke was working construction with Uncle Buddy and was sure Nate could get a job there as well.

We filled two steamer trunks with our belongings and shipped them along with my washing machine to Aunt Jean house. It was time for us to start a new life in a new city. We needed to settle someplace to give stability to our children. We felt that Detroit was a good choice since we had family there and jobs were plentiful. We packed up the kids and everything we could stuff into the car. We made a bed for the baby in the back window, put our three older children in the back seat and started the 3,000 miles drive to Detroit.

Thinking back to the days of my youth has given me much pleasure and I hope will shed some light on the history of my family and how far we have come and why we became a part of the Great Migration.

End

Printed in the United States
By Bookmasters